Reckless Ricardo

Book #18 of the Spirit of Truth Storybook Series

By Linda Mason

Reckless Ricardo
Book #18
The Spirit of Truth Storybook Series

Author: Linda C. Mason

Self published by:
Books By L Mason
P. O. Box 1162
Powhatan, VA 23139

LMasonOnTop@aol.com
www.BooksByLMason.com

ISBN-13: 978-1-5356-1661-4

Reckless Ricardo

"Leave me alone! I can play with those blocks if I want to! You can't stop me from taking them all or throwing them if I want to! Look, I can reach that window over there!" I declared as I threw the wooden block towards the window.

Smash! The window shattered with a loud crash as the teacher, Mrs. Winston, ran to make sure no other children were near it or got injured.

"Miss Carter, please take over the class while I take Ricardo out into the hall for a talk," Mrs. Winston said.

All the children in the classroom screamed and covered their ears but they were all safe.

We had just gotten back in class from lunch and I seemed wound up like a Yo-Yo. Mrs. Winston headed in my direction and I saw, by the look in her eyes, that she was pretty upset with me this time. I had disrupted her classroom all year with this kind of seemingly inconsiderate, thoughtless behavior and I think I might get kicked out of school after this episode. I just stood there with this *'I'm so sorry'* look on my face. She then cupped my arm and we headed for the principal's office.

As Mrs. Winston escorted me to the principal's office, I had a chance to think and reflect. This was the third time I had been reckless and careless with toys in her classroom this week. I'm sure she was out of solutions for redirecting my behavior by now. I don't know why I continue to be completely thought-less about those around me when I want to just throw things or treat my classmates as though no one mattered but me. Yesterday, I threw a chair at another child because she took a crayon from me. The other child jumped out of the way before the chair hit her. That could have had a terrible outcome.

I seem to either get very mad easily or I just wanted to play in a dangerous, reckless way with the toys around me.

This morning, after breakfast, I threw a chair from my front porch in front of the school bus as it stopped to pick me up. My dad was standing in the doorway but before he could get to me, I had done it. The bus driver put on brakes just in time but it did**n**'t make her very happy. She has threatened to put me off of the bus on more than one occasion. I have pulled some crazy reckless stunts on the bus as well.

"One more time, Ricardo! One more time!" she warned.

Dad and I lived to**g**ether with my grandmo**th**er. I never knew my mom because she went to live **in** heaven the day I was born. However, **G**randma and my dad did the be**s**t they could. I have been **f**rom doctor to doctor since I was four years old, and they haven't been able to figure **o**ut why I have been so **r**eckless all the time.

I am eight years old now, and I have no idea why I behave this way either. I don't want to hurt anyone. I don't want to be rude and thoughtless with other children. Reckless behavior just seems to run my life now more and more.

My dad has wanted to send me to this special basketball camp for the summer, but he's afraid that I will hurt someone or myself while there. He is not allowed to go with me and if I keep this up, I'll never get to go. I really do want to do things on my own for once. Why am I so thoughtless -- so reckless?

I sat in the main office with my head down. I knew Mr. Washington was tired of seeing me in there too. He finally called me to come into his private office. He looked at me and told me to lift up my head and talk to him. I looked into his eyes and with tears in my eyes, I said, "Sorry Mr. Washington." I wasn't afraid of Mr. Washington. He was a real cool principal but I was just sorry I could have hurt one of the kids while I was just playing.

"Ricardo," Mr. Washington continued, "Tell me what happened? Your grandmother is on her way to take you home, but first, tell me your story."

"Well, I was just playing with the blocks and all of a sudden, I just had to throw something. I guess I just made a silly decision and the block was in my hand, so I threw it," I explained even though I knew that was not only a bad excuse for throwing a wooden block inside a classroom with children all around, but there was no good excuse for throwing it hard enough to break a window pane.

"I'm so sorry," I said again as I lowered my head one more time.

"Raise your head up, Ricardo. I know you didn't mean to break the window. I want you to look at me."

I raised my head up and looked at Mr. Washington.

"Good, Ricardo," Mr. Washington continued.

"We have been through situations like this all year with you. Over the next few weeks, your teacher, your dad and I are going to sit down and figure out some different ways to help you. For now, I want you to spend some time at home with your family. Okay? I don't want anyone to get seriously hurt here, including you."

"But the Science Fair is coming up and I have been working on my project real hard, Mr. Washington," I said with defeat in my voice.

"Listen to me Ricardo," Mr. Washington said as he leaned forward and put his hand on my shoulder.

"What's been going on with you and **th**is repeated reckless behavior is more important than your Science **F**air project right now. I promise that you will get to finish the project, alright?"

"Yes sir," I said as the office secretary in**t**errupted and said my grandmother was here.

"Send Mrs. Morales in," Mr. Washington said.

As my grandma came **in**, she glanced at me sitting with tears still in my eyes.

"Are you alright?" she asked me with her slightly Spanish accent she still had from her past life in Costa Rica. She's been with us in America though since I was born, and I think she is doing well with English as a second language.

"Yes ma'am," I said unconvincingly.

"Would you please wait for us outside the door in the main office, Ricardo?" Mr. Washington asked, as he welcomed my grandmother and motioned for her to take a seat. He stood up to shake her hand.

As I shut the door behind me, I was thinking about just how tired I was with all of this. I sure hoped that all of them could figure out a way to help me, as Mr. Washington puts it, because I was getting exhausted behaving this way all the time. And the doctors certainly didn't seem to be able to figure anything out.

I really couldn't keep any friends either. The children at school were all afraid I'd hurt them and the kids in my neighborhood felt the same way. I played by myself most of the time and I had broken most of my toys at home, so I didn't have very much to play with anymore.

Now alone in my room at home, looking at all of my broken toys, I longed to have a normal childhood. My dad and Grandma were downstairs discussing me and my visit to the principal's office for the third time this week. I've already eaten dinner but instead of my usual peanut butter and jelly sandwich before bed, I had a cup of chicken noodle soup. I usually eat a peanut butter and jelly sandwich for breakfast as well and grandma packs me one for school lunch every day. It's my favorite food in the world but I didn't feel like eating one tonight, so I just didn't. I didn't deserve to eat my favorite food tonight.

I won't be going to school tomorrow or Friday. As a matter of fact, I won't be going next week either. I guess everyone will have to figure out what's going on in my head first, before I can return to school.

"I'm going to sleep... don't want to think about all of this anymore for tonight," I said out loud as I put my PJ's on and jumped into bed. I usually got into some kind of trouble every night before bed but tonight everything was peaceful.

In the morning, Grandma came in my room all excited about something. She woke me up and asked me to hurry down for breakfast. She said that she had a special *experiment* we were going to do together. It would be a different science project, and that I would be the star object for this special project. She then explained how she went on the internet last night while I was sleeping and read up on all kinds of allergic reactions people could have to different foods. She then asked me to trust her and stop eating peanut butter and jelly sandwiches for a week. We were going to record my behavior after every meal in which I didn't eat peanut butter and jelly.

I didn't like the idea at first because that was my favorite food in all the earth. However, she also said for every day I trusted her and didn't eat or sneak peanut butter and jelly, my dad would bring home a new toy for me.

"Oh, boy!" I said with renewed excitement **b**ecause all of my old toys had been broken up. This morning would be day one. I went through my first day without a reckless incident. I wasn't inconsid**e**rate that day at all to Grandma, either. I couldn't believe it! I can't re**m**ember a d**a**y without me ma**k**ing a mess of something at school or at home. A day without sassing Grandma or being just rude to her, was amaz**in**g! In the past, I seemed to just ruin everythin**g** I touched, or ruined the relationships I made with other children. No other families in the neighborhood ever invited me to their children's birthday parties, after I ruined one three years ago down the st**r**eet.

We wrote everything down that day. I was certainly hoping that all of these notes would reveal some good news even if the doctors couldn't figure all of this out.

When Dad came home, he had a toy train set for me. It was electric and so cool. He and I set it up together in my bedroom and I got to turn it on. It had special lights that turned on and off and bells that rang when it went through a certain station on the train tracks. I played with it all evening and didn't even want to come down for dinner.

Grandma pulled me away for some baked chicken and rice. I even had some steamed broccoli with melted cheese. I loved it! For dessert I had some coconut pie and then I took my bath and went to bed, staring at that train set until I went to sleep.

It **h**ad been day two and even though I missed my favor**i**te peanut butter and jelly sandwiches, I was looki**ng** forward to another possibly calm day. I was also looki**n**g forward to seeing Dad wh**e**n he came home because he **w**ould bring a ne**w** toy and I hadn't even destroyed the train set yet. Just as Grandma had promised, I had be**h**aved very well all day. No devastat**i**on at all around the house. We were both so happy. I almost didn't need another toy. It fe**l**t so good just to be and fe**e**l normal for a whole day. I didn't know what website she went to but I hope she remembers because maybe she could share with other parents in similar situations what she is doing with me. They may need answers, too.

When school let out the following day, even though I didn't go, I asked my grandma if I could invite one of my classmates over to see my train set. He lived two houses down from me. She said I could, so I ran outside and called out to Tony as he got off the bus.

"Hey Tony! Want to come over and see my new train set?"

"Really? You have a train set that is not broken?" He asked, looking really surprised.

"Sure do," I replied.

"I'll ask my mom and come right over if she says I can," Tony said as he ran into his house.

Ten minutes later, he was ringing the doorbell.

"It's me," Tony said.

"How are you doing here at home?"

"I'm doing much better, Tony."

"My grandma is trying an experiment with the foods I eat now, or should I say the foods I don't eat now. Well, anyway, I feel a lot better and I'm not reckless anymore with everything I touch. Isn't that great?" I said as we ran to my room.

Tony and I played with my train set for about thirty minutes and then he had to go home. I couldn't believe that I wasn't rude with Tony while he was there, and I could tell that he was just as surprised.

"My dad is bringing home a new **t**oy for me tonight. Would you like to come over tomorrow and see it, Tony?" I said, with a newly found confidence that I'd never had before.

Maybe I can now have real friends that I don't hurt or be rude to for no reason.

"Sure would," Tony said as he said goodb**y**e to me and my grandma. He then skipped out the door.

Well, as you can probably guess, this went **o**n for the rest of that week and the week after… having the same great results as we did immediately after I stopped eating the peanut butter and jelly sandwiches.

Months have passed now and dad doesn't b**u**y toys every day anymore but I really don't need them. Being calm and not reckless now was the biggest gift I could ever want anyway; although I do love having toys now that a**r**en't broken.

We all discovered along the way that it was the peanut butter making me behave like that, and not the jelly. I eventually did get to eat jelly sandwiches again, but Grandma and Dad looked real clo**s**e at labels on all the foods I ate after then.

They even sent a letter to school requesting that I not be given any products with peanut or peanut oil in them. And I began to receive the most stars on my chart in class. No one could believe the changes in my behavior. I began getting invitations to other children's birthday parties and everyone loved sitting near me in class. If I didn't know any better, I would think I was becoming the teacher's pet.

I ended up getting an 'A' on that new science project and now I have even more friends at school and at home. I think I'll find a way to keep all of that information my grandma gathered just in case the doctors might need help in the future.

My family chang**e**d doctors again and they told them what had made such a big change in my behavior. I don't think they really be**l**ieved her but it doesn't matter. We know what made a difference in my li**f**e ... and wow, what a life we have now! I can't believe why they didn't try the same experiment on me before we went through all of this. I could have still had all of those toys I destroyed.

Who knew that life could be so wonderful by just not eating peanut butter and jelly sandwiches?

Spirit of Truth Storybook Activity Page Instructions

1. *After reading the story, ask yourself the following questions:*

   - What did you like about the story?

   - What would you change about the story?

   - What could you have done to make things turn out differently? 

   - Can you think of a way to help others after reading this story?

2. *Go back through the story pages and **decode** your **secret message**.*

   - Write the message on the lines below.

   - Send it to me through email at: www.BooksByLMason.com 

I will send you back a personal comment. Be sure to include your gender and age.

Receive **15% discount coupon** off of the purchase of my Editor's Edition of "**The Spirit of Truth**" Storybook Series, with proof of purchase from A - Z. This special edition will contain all 26 stories within one volume along with some added goodies. Fill out the chart below and **please print** all information clearly.

A	B	C	D	E	F
G	H	I	J	K	L
M	N	O	P	Q	R
S	T	U	V	W	X
		Y	Z		

Dove Cut Out Letter

Glue your "*Dove Letter*" cutouts in the corresponding boxes, on top of the proper letter. Fill 26 spaces from A- Z. Then cut this page out and mail it to:

Linda Mason
P. O box 1162
Powhatan, VA 23139

Name: _______________________________________

Address: _____________________________________

State: _________   Zip: ____________

Email Address: ________________________________

During one of Ricardo's reckless days he was in front of the principal again.

Can you find the nine things that should not be there?

List the nine things that are out of place in the principal's office

1. ____

2. ____

3. ____

4. ____

5. ____

6. ____

7. ____

8. ____

9. ____

Principal's Office Answer Sheet

Radish

Necklace

Butterfly

Bug

Birthday hat

Pitch folk

Piñata

Ribbon

Sling shot

Instructions for Making Finger Puppets

1. Cut figures out. Follow the dotted line.

2. Cut strips out. Follow the dotted lines.

3. Fold over strip and tape into a ring.

4. Tape ring on the back of the figure that you cut out.

Cut Out the Finger Puppets

Cut Out the Finger Puppets

I Know! I Know!

r		t	g	l	h	b	o	y	t	n	r	e	c
i	i	e	u	u	h	y	y	a	t	t	d	g	h
a	k	k	p	l	l	e	m	m	t	n	b	d	h
y	g	u	i	n	u	u	a	k	j	m	j	h	e
f	f	d	d	e	l	e	r	N	r	v	U	v	b
w	s	d	h	j	n	i	k	m	c	n	n	h	b
a	s	w	e	t	z	c	a	z	d	n	x	v	d
c	z	s	u	y	f	n	t	o	t	g	r	g	n
D	x	w	O	f	w	G	c	b	i	r	b	n	h
y	J	m	k	a	b	r	p	r	y	a	u	t	n
z	x	e	c	e	s	r	g	e	h	m	h	g	r

__ _____ _____

___ ____ _____

___ _____ __

____ ____ ____

__ ________ __ __.

Find out *private* information about the author

Start at the blank rectangle. Then circle every third letter, not including the blank rectangle. Write those letters on the lines above to find out private information about the author. Find all **seven** *different true facts from seven different storybooks and send that information to me via my email at* LMasonOnTop@aol.com *and you will receive* **one storybook** *of your choice* **FREE**. *You only need to pay shipping and handling of $4.00. Don't forget to include your complete mailing address, your name and age. Have fun! (No answer key, so work hard).*

I Know! I Know!

b	g	M	r	r	y	e	e	f	w	q	i	q	w
r	e	t	s	h	n	t	h	g	b	g	f	o	d
x	r	v	n	n	m	p	i	y	t	s	r	e	n
v	b	a	n	o	m	f	w	e	e	g	d	d	f
T	a	c	a	w	f	a	v	n	a	f	r	r	e
a	b	c	d	e	f	g	h	i	j	k	l	m	n

BONUS

___ ___ _____________

_____ _____ ___

_________ ______________.

Start with the third letter and circle every third after that. Omit the last line. Have fun!

S.O.T. Message of Encouragement Worksheet

(You may copy this sheet)

(Fill in the missing letters on a <u>separate sheet of paper</u> or here, if you own the storybook, to unlock your secret message)

Reckless Ricardo

D _ _ ' _ _ p _ _ _ _ _ _ r _ _ _ _ _
y _ _ _ _ _ _ _ d _ s _ r _ _ i _ _
_ _ _ n _ s _ _ _ _ _ r _ _ s _ _ .
_ f _ h _ _ ' _ _ o _ _ _ _ s _ i _ _ ,
l _ _ _ _ _ t _ _ _ _ r _ e _ _ _ _ _
_ n _ _ l _ _ d _ _ t _ _ c _ _ _ _ .
A _ _ e _ _ t _ _ _ n , _ _ _ _ _ _
_ _ m _ k _ _ _ _ _ _ m _ _ _
s _ m _ _ h _ _ _ _ e _ w _ _ _ _
_ _ _ l _ _ _ g _ _ _ _ b _ _ _
_ _ _ r _ _ _ f .

Spirit of Truth Storybook Series

APPROPRIATE AGE LEVEL COLOR CODING KEY

The reading level for these stories is grade 5, but they can be understood and enjoyed by younger children, when read to them by older children or adults. The storybook covers have been colored to reflect the average comprehension levels for the following age groups.

Ages 4 and 5 = GREEN COVERS

Ages 6 and 7 = BLUE COVERS

Ages 8 and 9 = ORANGE COVERS

Ages 10 and above = RED COVERS

*A special inspirational message has been coded throughout each story to help create 'added focus,' as well as, a visual tool for interactive concentration. **Decode your secret message (written in red lettering throughout the story)** and send it to me, along with your name and age, through my personal email address on my website at www.BooksByLMason.com and you will receive a personal email response from me. Some of the letters of the secret message have already been provided to assist you in your decoding. Additionally, an added bonus finger puppet activity, brain games, puzzles or other goodies, awaits each reader in the back of every storybook. An added "Treasure Hunt" can be found throughout the illustrations from my collection of storybooks, **which details of this treasure hunt can only be found on my website.***

Also, E-Book Editions of this collection of storybooks, having no activities in the back of the books, as well as A Collector's Edition of this 26 Storybook Series is forthcoming. The collector's edition will include all 26 stories in the same book or 2 Volumes; at which time, the Master's List of every inspirational message will be revealed.

1. *Anxious Arlene:* This story is about an *anxious* family consisting of a young brother and sister who lives with their grandpa and grandma. They have a little adopted dog that was never claimed or found by the original owner, and they all live together (with a few mishaps), in a loving, exciting home. This story can be enjoyed by children ages five and up.

2. *Busy Benny:* This story is about a busy little boy who loves to tinker with Wacky car models. He gets the opportunity to create a child sized Wacky car, with the help of his mom and dad, and finally enters it into a race with him doing the driving. He runs into a little surprise during his test run. This story can be enjoyed by children ages seven and up.

3. *Catty Carla:* This story is about a group of neighborhood house cats who carry on 'catty' conversations behind their friend's back at times. One particular Burmese cat soon realizes that her behavior was not appropriate, and it could be a little late for apologies. This story deals with death portrayed through animal characters. This book is dedicated to my daughter, Tamara, who as an adult, loss a cat she adored, Dr. Jeckyl, to an illness. The story line is very light; however, use parental wisdom. This story can be enjoyed by children ages five and up.

4. *Doubtful Denise:* This story is about a single father raising a young teenaged daughter who is full of doubt about herself, her abilities, and her future. Through a father's persistent encouragement and unyielding love for her, she eventually gains trust in herself and finds hope for a brighter future. This story can be enjoyed by children ages seven and up.

5. ***Excited Ernesto****:* This story is about a teenaged boy overcoming a fear of riding roller coasters. He experiences some exciting events at the county fair with a buddy friend of his and his buddy's sister, Maria. She adds extra excitement for Ernesto because no one knew she would be there, and he has a secret crush on her. Join this exciting group of youth as they sample the tasty treats found at all State Fairs, and as they experience some of the thrills of riding a roller coaster for the first time. Ride along with Ernesto, as your heart races to the beat of his own. This story can be enjoyed by children ages seven and up.

6. ***Fearless Freddie****:* Freddie is a little boy who is very creative and willing to test out any new adventure, regardless of risk. He is always ready and willing to try dangerous stunts until one day it gets him into big trouble. Does he learn from making dangerous choices, or does he continue to believe he is *invincible?* This story can be enjoyed by children ages five and up.

7. ***Graceful Gregory****:* Gregory loves to dance. He encounters teasing by his peers, but continues to do what he loves. He eventually meets another little boy who is not so interested in dancing, but his family is insisting that he gives it a try. The two boys meet and things begin to change for both of them. This story can be enjoyed by children ages seven and up, but younger if the reader is already dancing.

8. ***Hopeful Henry****:* Henry is full of anticipation for the new school year and is hopeful he will not experience the disappointments he has had in the past. He apparently gets disappointed over, and over again until a tragedy occurs in his life and he ends up being supported by the very people he thought were insignificant. He learns also, not only to see things differently, but to always be grateful and remain hopeful. This story can be enjoyed by children ages seven and up.

9. *Itchy Irvin:* This story is played out using a pack of dogs as characters. One of them misjudges some physical symptoms of another dog, and begins teasing him. That dog gets picked on constantly because of a skin condition. This particular *pack of dogs* meets a little boy who is going through a similar situation with his classmates at school. Let's see how this doggy story barks out. This story can be enjoyed by children ages seven and up.

10. *Jumping Josey:* This story is about a teenager who lives a life of thrills, while flipping and jumping, every chance she gets. She ultimately gets to experience one of her life's dreams -- sky diving. Travel with Josey as she goes on the most exhilarating jump of her life. This story can be enjoyed by children ages seven and up.

11. *Kissing Kirkland:* This story is about a very affectionate little boy who spends his days and nights kissing all kinds of creatures. Eventually, his normal kissing routine lands him into big trouble when he gets attacked by a momma duck. Let's follow our adorable *Kissing Kirkland* through an average day at home and see how he survives some of the repercussions having a personality like this, may present. This story can be enjoyed by children ages five and up.

12. *Lonely Lucilia:* This story is about two teenagers that are best friends. They are forced to separate, due to a family relocation, to a different country. The storyline starts out in a coastal town in Fife, Scotland, where Lucilia and Dillard have lived all of their lives. Take this lonesome journey with Lucilia, as she is forced to move from the only place she's ever known, and from her very best friend in the world, to a strange country she knows nothing about -- the United States of America. This story can be enjoyed by children ages eight and up.

13. *Muddy Maria:* This story explores the life of a little girl who loves to get dirty. With the help of her creative mother, her *dirty,* playful habit is channeled into a very productive

fun activity. Dive in to this interesting twist of events and discover how playing in a lot of dirt, in some situations, can possibly turn out to be good for you. This story can be enjoyed by children ages five and up.

14. *Noisy Nelly:* This story explores the hatching of a bird from a bird's perspective. As this special bird explores her new world, words of wisdom flow from its mother. These words eventually take root in Nelly's heart in a very unique way. Soar with Nelly as she learns a very important lesson by refocusing her perspective on a part of her life she once perceived as gloomy. This story is dedicated to my first grandchild, Niyah Nylliana Mason, whom I believe one day will also soar as high as an eagle. This story can be enjoyed by children ages seven and up.

15. *Orphaned Ophelia:* Most of this story takes place in a very unique orphanage. Ophelia lives with the discomforts of not having a traditional family, but through it all she finds the compassion to help others. One day that compassion is returned, and she receives the most rewarding surprise of her life. This story can be enjoyed by children ages five and up.

16. *Pudgy Pete:* This story is about a little boy who obviously, because of his nickname, carries a little more weight than the average child. Journey with Pete as his self-pity and low self-esteem evolves into self-worth. After befriending a new *physically challenged* neighbor who moves in next door, she teaches him how to appreciate the special person he is, and not to focus on what size pants he wears. This story can be enjoyed by children ages seven and up.

17. *Quarrelsome Quaniqua:* This story contains **sensitive** material. It is not intended to be read as a *bedtime* story. Our story deals with a serious issue that some children must live with every day: ***an abusive living environment*** (non-sexual). The main character is a Latino teen (Quaniqua) who lives in poor, none-nurturing conditions. She becomes bitter and

her behavior follows suit, until she meets someone outside of the home, and of a different culture, who finally treats her with respect. This causes Quaniqua to pull herself up and out of the pit she seemed to be falling into. Hang in there with her through the hard times, and see this young lady become a more productive, happier citizen. This story can be enjoyed by children eight and up; however, use parental wisdom as to if this story is suited for your particular younger child.

18. ***Reckless Ricardo:*** This story is about a young boy who starts out with some very reckless and disrespectful behaviors, but ends up with a very unusual science project that helps him start behaving in new, more respectful ways. You might be surprised at the results of this nontraditional outcome to a very common allergy. This story can be enjoyed by children ages seven and up.

19. **Shy Stanley***:* This story is about a very quiet little boy who has some very interesting talents. He spends a lot of his time alone; however, he is extremely observant. Stanley meets a little girl with similar gifts and interests, which creates a bond that opens them both up to view their world differently. Let's visit these interesting young people and discover what their talents are. Maybe you have similar talents as well, and might have some interesting ideas of your own as to how to present those talents to the world. This story can be enjoyed by children ages seven and up.

20. **Tearful Tanya:** This story deals with a little girl who is full of grief over the passing of her grandmother. The family has a spiritual upbringing, and the little girl's mom guides her through the grieving process as she draws strength from above, where she's convinced her grandmother now resides. This story may be a little sensitive if you are a child in a similar situation, yet it can be enjoyed by children ages five and above.

21. **Ungrateful Ursula**: This story contains '**sensitive**' material. It is recommended for children ages ten and above. The story deals with a teenaged girl who grew up without her mother, and who very rarely saw her father. She lives temporarily with her aging grandmother. However, because of her grandmother's illness, Ursula must now live with her father, and she begins to use '*cutting*' as her method of coping. Things smooth out, but it's a very bumpy, painful ride. Walk with Ursula as she moves from '*much pain*' to '*much gain.*' This story can be enjoyed and read by children ages ten and above.

22. **Valiant Vivica**: This story is about a very gifted little girl who loves contact sports. Boys her same age seem to both admire her, and can be intimidated by her unprecedented strength at the same time. A natural disaster occurs on the day of Vivica's first wrestling tournament, and her valiant personality takes over. Follow along as she demonstrates extraordinary acts of bravery, and through it all, this experience will change her forever. This story can be enjoyed by children ages eight and above.

23. **Worrying Winston**: This story is about a little boy whose mother is an active Marine in the United States' Armed Forces. Winston is a very responsible little boy; however, he does worry a great deal about his mother's well-being. While on a *Treasure Hunt*, a game designed by his mother using riddles written in a letter Winston received, an unfortunate accident occurs and his mother ends up with a serious injury. Will they complete the Treasure Hunt*?* Stand with Winston and his father as they draw strength from each other to deal with a life's situation that changes their entire world. This story can be enjoyed by children ages eight and above.

24. **X-Con Xavier**: This story has been presented in '*limerick style poetry*' to lighten the seriousness of the topic for a child. Because of Xavier's destructive behavior, he is placed

in various state institutions. Xavier meets a person while incarcerated that offers him hope and a different way of thinking. His inner spiritual change eventually points him in a new direction. Now with new hope, he has a chance to begin a new, more productive lifestyle outside of lock-up. This story can be enjoyed and read by children ages ten and above.

25. **Yearning Yolanda**: This story takes you on a short journey with a twelve year old young girl who lost her eyesight in a car accident a year ago. She yearns for life to be as it was before the accident; however, life has a way of throwing you constant challenges that could cause you to either withdraw further into bitterness, or to emerge with a heart of gratefulness. Which one will Yolanda choose? Walk with Yolanda through an even harder challenge that, if handled with fear and bitterness, could not only take her life, but the lives of her mother and her best friend, Toby (her dog). This story can be enjoyed by children ages eight and above.

26. **Zealous Zeporah**: Zeporah is a very passionate young lady full of enthusiasm for life. She jogged regularly, but one day she slipped and fell injuring her ankle. A situation such as this would have brought most people to a halt, or perhaps could cause others to go into a state of temporary depression. How will Zeporah handle a situation like this, when so many people are depending on her enthusiasm to help motivate them? This story can be enjoyed by children ages seven and above.

About The Author

Minister Linda Mason is a unique ministry gift to the Body of Christ. Her experiences include the establishment of *Spirit of Praise Liturgical Outreach, Inc.*, a non-profit 501 © 3 organization, which not only helped to establish and over- see new dance ministries, but also extended into the communities.

In addition to the *Spirit of Truth Storybook Series*, Minister Linda has published *Appetizers from the Word of God... Are You Hungry?* Volumes 1, 2, & 3; which is an awesome tool for teach- ing foundational truths, in a simplistic manner, from God's Word.

Linda is a native of Suffolk, Virginia, the wife of George B. Mason, Jr., the mother of three; Tamara, Tiena, and George III. She has three adorable grandchildren, Niyah, Laana, and Aaron. Linda holds an Associate Degree in Early Childhood Education and has a passion for writing. She has written and is in the process of publishing these 26 children's stories from A to Z. Additionally Linda has written an exciting suspense novel series for young adults; Beyond Your Control, Disappointment Meets Grace, Within My Reach, followed by many more. Her plan is to have these unique stories available in E-Books, Audiobooks and paperbacks in the near future.

What others have stated about this Series

- *Author Linda Mason's book, "Kissing Kirkland", is one of a series of books that tells a delightful story with a secret hidden valuable message for children. Her stories will captivate her audience with a variety of age appropriate activities to enhance each child's learning. As an educator for many years, I highly recommend her books!* **By Amelia Hopkins, a high school counselor.**

- *Linda Mason has done an excellent job using her creativity and insight in writing this series of books, **Spirit of Truth Storybook Series from A-Z**. Each book deals with a subject or situation, such as a particular disability, or set-back that a child might encounter and have difficulty dealing with. The books offer resolutions that are positive and encouraging, helping a child build strength, confidence and maturity. The activities in the back of each book reinforce the lesson learned. The graphics are colorful and eye-catching, and each book's vocabulary is age appropriate. Each book is color coded to fit each age group, so there are appropriate books for every child's age. These are books your children will want to read or hear over and over; read by a big sister or brother. And they also have the opportunity to communicate with the author directly! I highly recommend these books for your children sand grandchildren!* **By Nona J. Mason, a retired teacher, mother and grandmother.**